jj Mayer, Mercer and Marianna
      Mayer
      One frog too many

DATE DUE			
FE 12 '87	DE 1 '92		
MR 26 '87	JAN 17 '95		
AP 29 '87			
MY 26 '87			
DE 4 '87			
JA 27 '88			
FE 4 '88			
MR 29 '88			
SE 29 '88			
OC 6 '88			
NO 10 '88			
NO 29 '88			
JE 5 '89			
DE 10 '90			

ONE FROG TOO MANY

by Mercer
and Marianna Mayer

Dial Books for Young Readers
New York

Copyright © 1975 by Mercer and Marianna Mayer. All rights reserved.
Library of Congress Catalog Card Number: 75-6325
First Pied Piper Printing 1977
Printed in Hong Kong by South China Printing Co.
C O B E
4 6 8 10 9 7 5 3
A Pied Piper Book is a registered trademark of Dial Books for Young Readers
A division of E. P. Dutton | A division of New American Library
® TM 1,163,686 and ® TM 1,054,312
ONE FROG TOO MANY is published in a hardcover edition by
Dial Books for Young Readers, 2 Park Avenue, New York, New York 10016
ISBN 0-8037-6734-X

For Phyllis Fogelman
who got the ball rolling

... Hats off to you